PIGS from A to Z

PIGS from A to Z

ARTHUR GEISERT

Houghton Mifflin Company

Boston

For my parents, Leonard and Doris Geisert

Library of Congress Cataloging-in-Publication Data

Geisert, Arthur
  Pigs from A to Z.

  Summary: Seven piglets cavort through a landscape of
hidden letters as they build a tree house.
  [1. Alphabet. 2. Pigs—Fiction. 3. Tree houses—Fiction]
I. Title.
PZ7.G2724Pi 1986   [E]   86-18542
ISBN 0-395-38509-1   PAP ISBN 0-395-77874-3

For information about this and other Houghton Mifflin
trade and reference books and multimedia products,
visit The Bookstore at Houghton Mifflin on the
World Wide Web at http://www.hmco.com/trade/ .

Printed in the United States of America

HOR 10 9 8 7 6 5 4 3 2

Make Way for Piglets!

———

In this ABC, seven little pig siblings cavort through a landscape of hidden letters, looking to build the perfect tree house. They build, they rest, they play, and they build some more.

The careful reader will find each letter of the alphabet in the intricate etchings. Occasionally one or more of the little pigs will try to hide, but always seven piglets and five forms of a letter will appear on each page. In addition to seven pigs and five forms of the featured letter, one form of the preceding letter and one form of the following letter are hiding. For example, on the page for the letter D, there are five D's, one C, one E, and seven piglets.

This is a story and a puzzle as well as an alphabet created to challenge the eye and mind of every reader. For those who wish to check their abilities, a key at the back of the book will reveal the hidden letter shapes for each page. But no fair looking ahead.

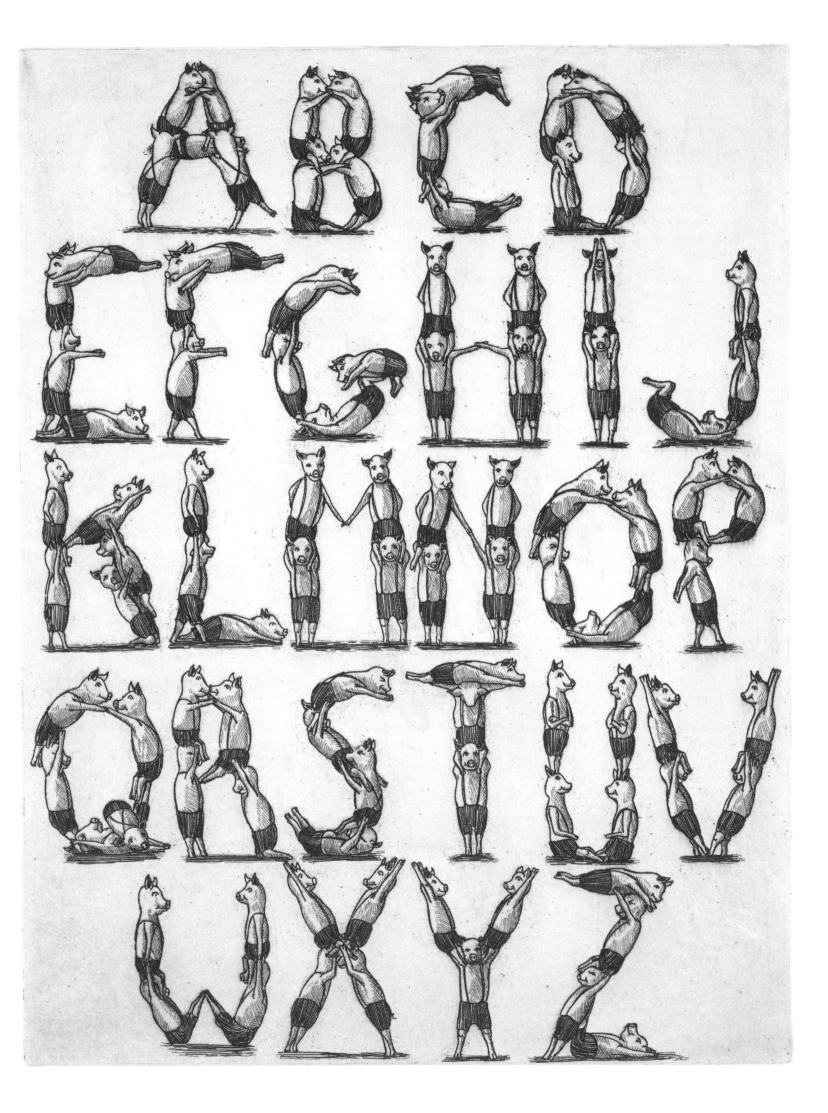

A is for apples to eat in the morning. The perfect way to start a day of tree house building.

B is for big bites of apples. Then off to work, chopping down the birch tree.

C is for chores: cutting countless cords of wood — cheerfully.

D is for dragging the lumber. Dragging was drudgery.

E is for the eerie forest. It was scary.

F is for floating down the river. The water felt fresh and good.

G is for getting the lumber over the gorge.

H is for a game of hide-and-seek.
Where are the seven piglets?

I is for the ideal tree.

J is for juggling boards for the tree house joists.

K is for kicking over the nail keg.
A small catastrophe.

L is for lunchtime. Lower the ladder!

M is for making music—or just noise?

N is for napping neatly in rows.

O is for ouch, ouch, ouch, ouch, ouch, ouch, ouch, and oink, oink, oink, oink, oink, oink, oink.

P is for photograph. A portrait of the piglets and their perfect tree.

Q is for a quiet game of croquet before getting back to work.

R is for raising the rafters.

S is for shingling. The view was spectacular.

T is for topping out. The piglets have finished.

U is for unwinding. Upside-down was not unusual.

V is for the voyage home across the vast gorge.

W is for washing clothes in a wind-powered washing machine.

X is for extra bracing and for giving Pa some expert help.

Y is for yawn.

Z is for ZZZZZZZ.

A time to dream about tomorrow.

Key

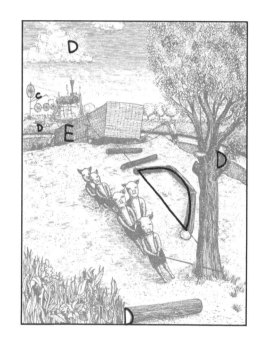

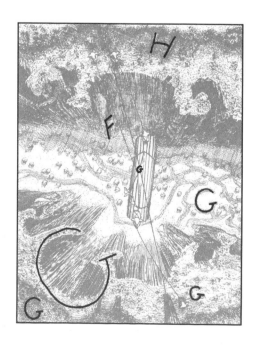

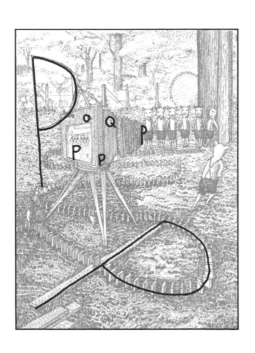

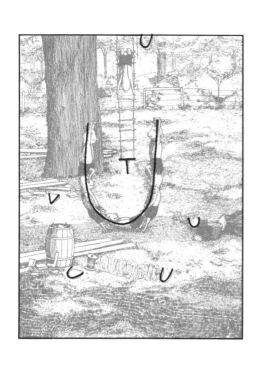